PINKFONG: BABY SHARK AND THE POLICE SHARKS!
A CENTUM BOOK 978-1-912841-64-6
Published in Great Britain by Centum Books Ltd.
This edition published 2018.
3 5 7 9 10 8 6 4 2

Original Korean edition first published by Smart Study Co., Ltd.

This edition published by Centum Books Ltd in 2018 by arrangement with Smart Study Co., Ltd.

Centum Books Ltd, 20 Devon Square, Newton Abbot, Devon, TQ12 2HR, UK.

books@centumbooksltd.co.uk

CENTUM BOOKS Limited Reg. No. 07641486.

A CIP catalogue record for this book is available from the British Library.

Printed in China.

pinkfong

BABY SHARK
STORYBOOK SERIES

Baby Shark and the Police Sharks!

centum

Baby Shark Family & Friends

Baby Shark

Baby Shark lives under the ocean and is curious about everything around him. He likes to sing. When he's scared, he sings to help him feel brave.

Mummy Shark

There are no limits to the things that Mummy Shark can do! She always listens to Baby Shark and they share a very special bond.

Daddy Shark

Daddy Shark is a strong and mighty hunter. He is much more than just Baby Shark's father though, the two of them play together like best friends!

The Octopus Sisters

The Octopus Sisters have a total of sixteen arms, so it's no wonder that they get tangled together so often!

Hammerhead Shark

Hammerhead Shark has a unique head shape! He lives inside a very old and big sunken ship.

Grandma Shark

Grandma Shark likes to read. She is a kind and thoughtful grandma who always has time to spend with Baby Shark.

Grandpa Shark

Grandpa Shark is wise and smart. He is famous for his hot clam buns and he loves to share his love of cooking with Baby Shark.

Baby Shark and Daddy Shark are patrolling the ocean.
'Police Sharks on duty! We keep the peace in the ocean!' says Baby Shark.

Suddenly, a loud, wailing siren goes off and the Police Sharks hear the cry for help.

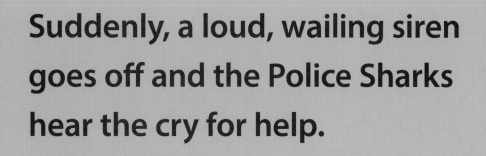

Eeeeeee!

Eeeeeee!

The Police Sharks start swinging their tails back and forth and quickly head in the direction of the siren. They are on their way to help!

The Police Sharks see someone peeking out from some coral. It is a fish family frantically flapping their fins.

'Police Sharks, thank Neptune you're here! The Octopus Sisters are fighting!'

'There's nothing to fear . . . the Police
Sharks are here!' says Baby Shark.
'Sisters, sisters, no fighting in the ocean!'
says Daddy Shark.

'We aren't fighting,' say the Octopus Sisters. 'We just got tangled up in the darkness!'

'We'll untangle you!'

The Police Sharks get straight to work.

Daddy Shark untangles one sister's arms and Baby Shark untangles the other.

Finally, they manage to part the two sisters.
'Thank you, Police Sharks!' say the
Octopus Sisters.

'Let's high-fin,
Baby Shark!'

16

But all of a sudden, the siren
starts to wail again.
'We're on our way!'

Eeeeeee!

Eeeeeee!

'No ocean is too deep
for the Police Sharks!'

'Over here, Police Sharks! Come quickly,' say some small fish as they gasp in horror. 'Someone has broken into Hammerhead Shark's house!'

'Help!'

'You're surrounded by the Police Sharks!' shouts Daddy Shark.

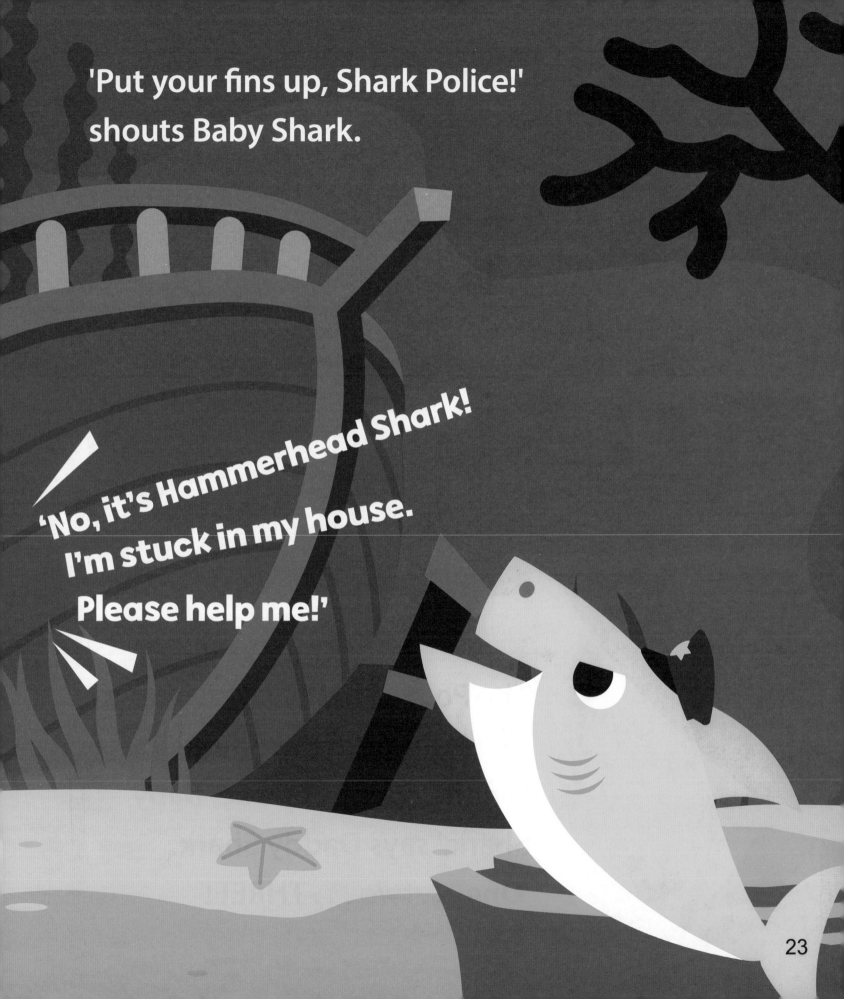

'Put your fins up, Shark Police!'
shouts Baby Shark.

'No, it's Hammerhead Shark!
I'm stuck in my house.

Please help me!'

The Police Sharks swim over to
pull Hammerhead Shark out.
'On the count of three, Baby
Shark,' says Daddy Shark.
'One . . . two . . . THREE!'

They safely pull Hammerhead
Shark out of the hole.
'I'm finally free! Thank you
so much!' says Hammerhead
Shark.

'Can't be beat, doo-doo-doo-doo-doo!'
'Task complete, doo-doo-doo-doo-doo!'

Who will the Police Sharks help now?

Eeeeeee! Eeeeeee!

There's no need to panic, the siren is sounding to start the award ceremony for the Police Sharks! 'Put your hands together for the best Police Sharks ever!' says Hammerhead Shark. 'Congratulations and thanks for keeping the peace!' say the Octopus Sisters.

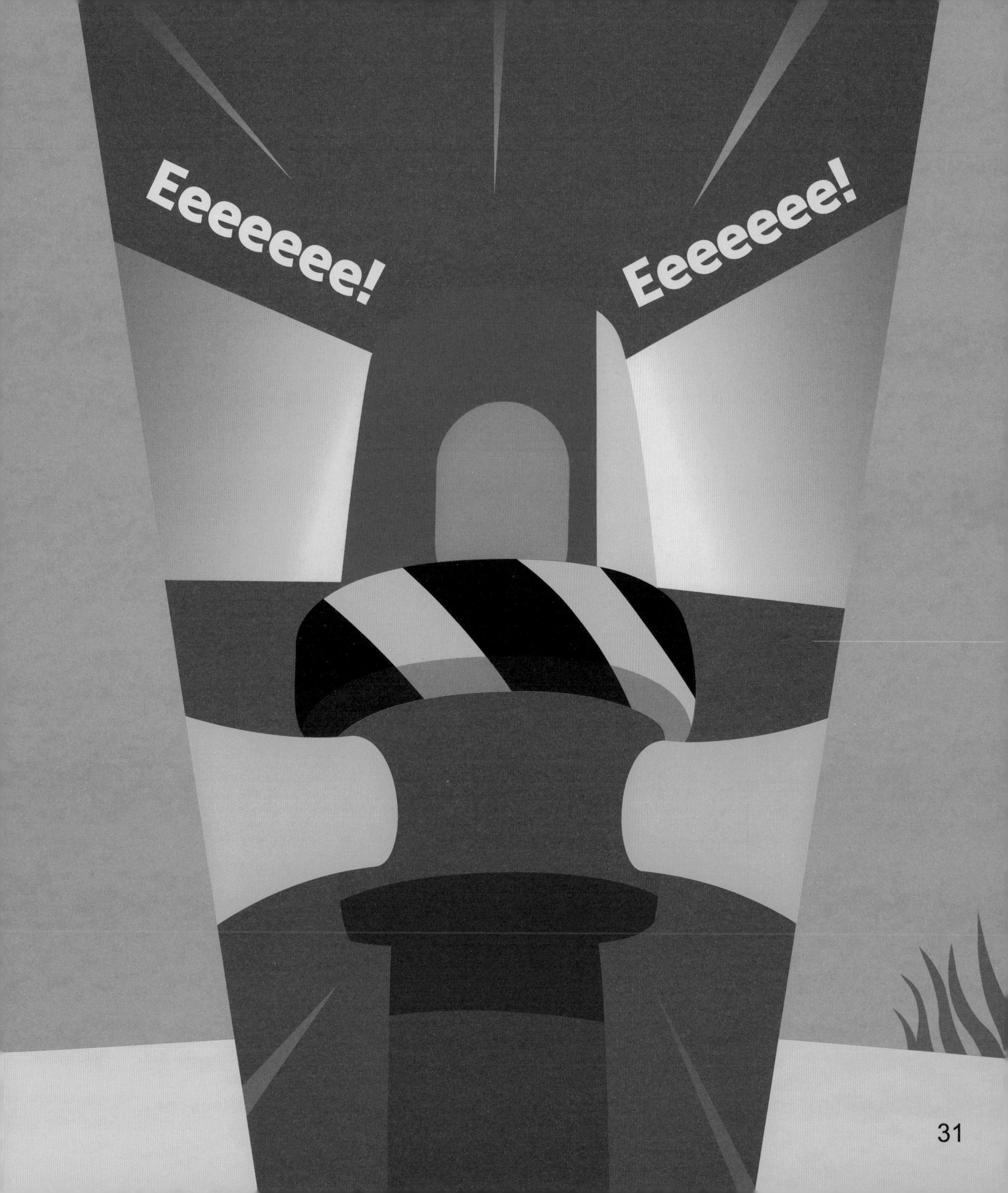
Eeeeeee!
Eeeeeee!